To Sue, forever.

Richard Torrey

Almost

HarperCollinsPublishers

My name is Jack.
I am almost six.

That is almost grown up.

I can almost wear big clothes . . .

and ride a big bike.

Almost.

I can almost make my own breakfast.

I almost like vegetables—except for beans, carrots, spinach, peas, corn. . . .

I can almost build a real robot.

That's why I'm almost thinking of being a scientist . . .

or a baseball player.

I'm almost the best on my team. Once I almost hit the winning home run.

And I'm almost the best at karate.
Yesterday I almost flipped my
instructor, Mr. Woo.

I almost never get scared.

I almost never cry.

Because I'm almost six.
And that is almost grown up.

Almost.